MW01078892

Max Meets a Bully

Written by: Mena Buscetto
Illustrated by: Paul Santiago

2017 Liberty Whale Press

Written by: Mena Buscetto
Illustrated by: Paul Santiago
Designed by: Jamie Laliberte Whalen M.A.

Published by Liberty Whale Press,.
LWP 2017

DEDICATION

To my Nonna, the epitome of friendship, love and kindness.

Love,
Mena

Max, Jenny, and Kevin were very best friends.

They all lived in the same neighborhood, on the same street.

They all played together every day after school and on weekends.

They all went to Mountain Peak Elementary School and were all in Ms. Holly's class.

Max, Jenny, and Kevin always shared their snack in the morning.

Kevin would give Max his peanut butter crackers, Max would give Jenny his Oreos, and Jenny would give Kevin her cheese puffs.

At recess, Kevin was always the captain for the kickball game and always picked Jenny and Max for his team first.

Every day on the bus Max, Kevin, and Jenny took the only three-person seat and played many intense games of Rock,

Paper, Scissors, until they reached the bus stop.

They were very best friends and nothing could ever separate them.

Or so they thought.

It was a Tuesday morning when Ms. Holly announced to the class that she had exciting news.

"Class, listen up! Today a new student will be coming to join our class!" Ms. Holly said.

Max, Jenny, and Kevin looked at each other with excitement.

Before Ms. Holly could say anything else, a girl walked into the classroom.

She was wearing a bright pink dress and white sandals with sunflowers on them.

Her dark brown hair was perfectly curled and a giant pink bow sat on top of her head.

"My name is Galina Miller," the new girl said, "and I just moved here from the city."

From that moment on, every kid at Mountain Peak Elementary School wanted to be friends with Galina Miller.

Galina wore the prettiest pink clothes and always had her hair curled perfectly, complete with a pink ribbon. She told the most exciting stories about living in the city, and always had yummy food to share at snack time (mostly because she was never satisfied with what her mother packed).

Max wasn't impressed, but Jenny and Kevin thought Galina was the coolest girl in school.

That day, Galina invited Jenny and Kevin to sit with her at morning snack.

When Max tried to join them, Galina turned away and said, "Sorry, there's only room for three!"

Max looked to Jenny and Kevin for help, but they just shrugged and turned back to talk to Galina. Max sat alone.

At recess, Galina demanded to be team captain and have first pick for the kickball game.

Everyone agreed.

She chose Jenny and Kevin for her team, but not Max.
Soon, Max was standing all alone.

"Sorry, Max. Looks like nobody wants you for their team!" Galina giggled and skipped away towards the kickball field.
Kevin laughed and ran after her.

Jenny looked back at Max sadly, but ran after them too.

Max was very sad and went to play on the swing set alone, while his friends laughed and played kickball without him.

This became the new routine, and Max found himself alone all the time.

One day at recess, when Max was the last one to be picked for kickball again, he decided he had had enough.

"Why do you never pick me Galina? I'm great at kickball. You haven't even given me a chance!"

Galina laughed and put her hands on her hips. "Because, you can't possibly be good at kickball Max. You probably can't even see the ball!" she said, pointing to his thick, black framed glasses.

Max's face turned bright red as everyone started pointing and laughing at his glasses.
Galina walked away, looking very proud as Max backed away slowly.

On the bus ride home, Jenny and Kevin let
Galina sit in Max's seat.
Max had to sit all alone.

Max was tired of how mean Galina was to him, and even more upset that Jenny and Kevin weren't being very good friends.

He decided to get help from Ms. Holly.
After he told her the whole story, Ms. Holly called Galina into the classroom from recess.

Galina skipped in with a huge smile on her face.
"Galina, Max is telling me that you aren't being very nice to him lately. Is that true?"

Galina's eyes widened. Max's face turned bright red. He looked down at his shoes.

"I just didn't pick Max for my team for kickball," she said ever so sweetly. She turned to Max.
"I'm sorry if I hurt your feelings Max." Max froze. He didn't know what to say.

"That's okay," Max said softly.
Ms. Holly looked pleased and said "Good girl Galina. Now you two go out and play."
Galina turned and skipped back out of the room gleefully.

Max followed with the hope that Galina would finally be nice to him, but the minute they were outside and out of Ms. Holly's sight, Galina stuck out her foot and tripped Max, sending him sprawling out on the grass.

Everyone pointed and laughed as Galina ran to Jenny and Kevin laughing, and Max tried his hardest not to cry.

The next day at recess, Max sat off to the side while teams were picked for kickball.

He played with the blades of grass and pretended not to notice when Galina began yelling his name.

"What's wrong Max? Too afraid to play against REALLY good kickball players? Chicken! Chicken!" She said, pointing at him.

Max had had enough.
He stood and walked right up to Galina.

All of the other kids on the playground froze.
They watched very quietly, not knowing what was
going to happen next.

"I just don't want to play today Galina. I never
get picked to play and always end up sitting on
the side by myself anyway.

It's not nice to leave people out of games, keep
their friends away from them, and call them
names. I want you to please
say you're sorry."

Galina started laughing. Soon, everyone on the
playground was laughing along with her.
Max's face turned red and he looked down to the
ground, ready to run right back into Ms. Holly's
classroom.

Suddenly, Max heard Jenny's voice above all the laughter.

"He's right. All you've done since you got to this school is pick on Max. It isn't fair. He just wants to be your friend.

He's really cool and you never even gave him a chance." Jenny walked over and stood next to Max.

"If you can't be nice and say you're sorry, then I can't be friends with you anymore, Galina." Jenny said confidently.

Kevin stood there timidly, not quite knowing what to do next. He looked around at everyone staring at what was
happening, then quickly ran to join Max and Jenny.
"That goes for me too." Kevin said.

Galina, who looked a little more nervous now, let out another laugh.

"Fine. It doesn't matter, I have plenty of friends." Galina looked around, expecting some of the other kids on the playground to come join her, but nobody did.

Everyone went back to playing their games, leaving Galina in the middle of the kickball field.
Galina was now the one who stood all alone.

"We want to be your friend Galina. But you need to say you're sorry to Max."

Galina looked at the ground and began to cry.

"All the kids at my old school who acted like this had the most friends. I was nervous about coming here and not knowing anyone, so I thought that would work. I'm sorry Max."

Max walked over to Galina.

"That's not the way to make friends, Galina.

You make friends by being nice to other people, not by making fun of them or making them feel bad."

Galina nodded. "I'll try, I promise."

"You have first pick Galina!" Yelled someone from across the playground.

With all the excitement, Max had almost forgotten a game was about to begin. He started to walk away towards the swing set.

"I pick Max," Galina said confidently. Max spun around, not believing what he had just heard.

Not only was he picked first but GALINA had picked him for her team!

He walked back over to her and she gave him a high five.

Their team won the game.

From that day on Galina, Max, Jenny, and Kevin all shared their snacks with each other.

They decided not to sit in the three person seat on the bus anymore.

They even played after school and every weekend at each other's houses.

They were kind to each other and most importantly, always picked each other for kickball.

About the Author

Mena Buscetto is a student at Marist College studying English, Adolescent Education, Theatre and Creative Writing. Mena is from Waterford, Connecticut and enjoys singing, dancing, reading and writing fiction. She hopes to become a teacher and continue writing books about topical issues in schools.

Made in the USA
Middletown, DE
30 May 2017